MY
BIRTHDAY LAND
ADVENTURE

This book
was especially written
for
Augusta Maclean
with love
from
Grandpa Tiree

Written by Margaret Gibson
Illustrated by Ester Kasepuu

Augusta Maclean awoke with a big smile on her face.

'Today is my birthday,' she said to herself. 'I wonder if there'll be any surprises?'
She slipped out of bed - and there was the very first surprise!
An enormous envelope was leaning against the end of her bed. Augusta peered closely at three mysterious words:

From Birthday Land

FROM BIRTHDAY LAND

Augusta Maclean
The Rectory
Ardconnel Terrace
Oban
Argyll Uk

Augusta excitedly opened the envelope and reached inside. Her fingers touched a large card. Carefully she pulled it out and this is what she read:

**Today's birthday girl
Augusta Maclean
is invited
to visit
Birthday Land
to find
her special birthday party
at the end of the rainbow.**

'Birthday Land! The end of the rainbow!' Augusta whispered to herself. 'How will I ever find them?' She walked over and opened the door. Stretching from her feet, far up into the sky, was a rainbow.

'Well,' said a very surprised Augusta. 'This must be the start of the rainbow. And what a red rainbow! I can hardly see the other colours.' Augusta put her foot onto the rainbow. It was very slippery!

'How do I climb up?' she wondered.
A small voice whispered into Augusta's ear:

'You can slide up and down rainbows or you can fly over them.'

And there, flying out of each colour band of the rainbow were seven beautiful butterflies: Violet, Indigo, Blue, Green, Yellow, Orange and Red. They were pulling a leaf by long gossamer threads.

'Sit on our leaf and hold on tightly,' said
Yellow Butterfly, 'and we will take you
to Birthday Land.'

'But I'm far too big for such a tiny leaf,'
said Augusta, 'and I would like Hector,
Angus and Caitlin to come with me.' Green
Butterfly shook her head. 'Only the birthday
child can visit Birthday Land.' To Augusta's
surprise she fitted quite snugly on the leaf
and soon they were gliding up the arc of the
rainbow towards the blue sky.

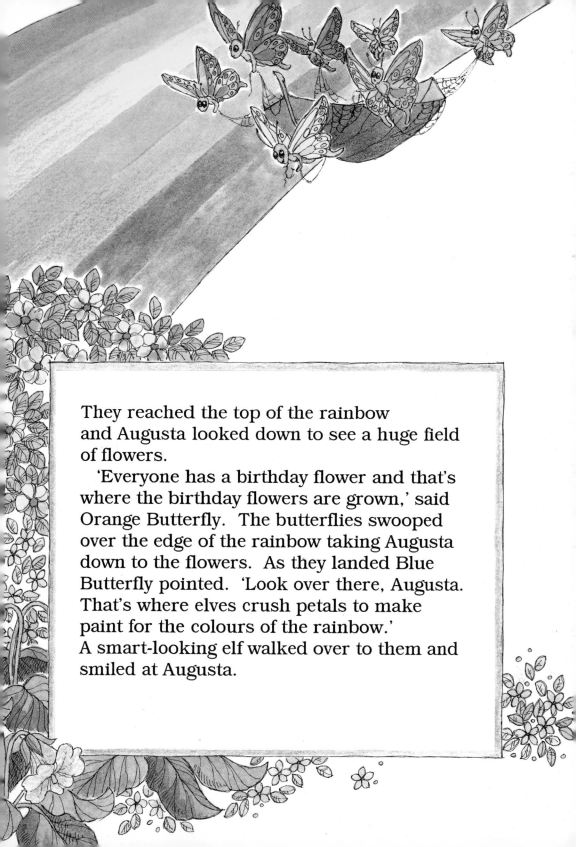

They reached the top of the rainbow
and Augusta looked down to see a huge field
of flowers.

'Everyone has a birthday flower and that's
where the birthday flowers are grown,' said
Orange Butterfly. The butterflies swooped
over the edge of the rainbow taking Augusta
down to the flowers. As they landed Blue
Butterfly pointed. 'Look over there, Augusta.
That's where elves crush petals to make
paint for the colours of the rainbow.'
A smart-looking elf walked over to them and
smiled at Augusta.

'Ah, today's special birthday girl,' said
the elf. 'Today is October 29th, so your
birthday flower is the calendular.'
He handed Augusta a tiny pot wrapped in
birthday paper.

'I have planted a calendular for you. When
you return home you must unwrap it, put it
in a sunny spot and give it water.'

'Thank you very much,' said Augusta.
'Could you please tell me why you've
painted so much red on the rainbow?'
The elf looked unhappy. 'It's not our paint,
Augusta,' he said. 'The dragon who guards
the birthstones is upset about something.
He is breathing fire and it's turning the
rainbow red.'

'Now we must visit the dragon to collect
Augusta's present,' said Indigo Butterfly.
'The dragon leaves a special stone for each
birthday child at the entrance to his cave.'
As the butterflies towed her back into
the sky, Augusta waved goodbye to the elf.
Then she noticed a little card on her birthday
flower pot which read:

'Before you reach the rainbow's end
The birthstone dragon must be your friend'

'This is very strange. Whatever does it
mean?' wondered Augusta.

Violet Butterfly smiled. 'Everyone in
Birthday Land is hoping that today's
special birthday child can find out
what is making the dragon so unhappy.
His red breath is spoiling the rainbow.'

'When we reach the dragon's cave we will collect your stone. Then we'll try to find some way to make the dragon happy and stop the red mist in the rainbow,' said Blue Butterfly. 'The dragon stays deep inside his cave. He hasn't seen a child for a long time.'

Augusta held on tightly to the edges of the leaf as they followed the rainbow downwards.

'Where is the dragon's cave?' she asked. 'All I can see is lots of red mist.'

Green Butterfly called out: 'Look carefully down through the mist, Augusta. Can you see the great mountain of rocks? That's where the dragon lives.' They turned downwards pulling a very excited Augusta towards the mountain. They gently landed near the entrance to a large cave. The butterflies looked for Augusta's birthstone but it was nowhere to be seen!

The butterflies talked quietly amongst
themselves, then Yellow Butterfly asked
Augusta,
   'Are you brave enough to find the dragon
and ask him why he is spoiling the rainbow?'
Augusta took a deep breath and nodded, but
she had a little thought inside her head:
   'I wish Hector, Angus and Caitlin were with
me and I would feel much braver.'
She stood up and walked slowly through
the red mist into the dark cave.
Augusta heard a loud grumbling noise.
She turned a corner and there in front
of her was the enormous dragon!

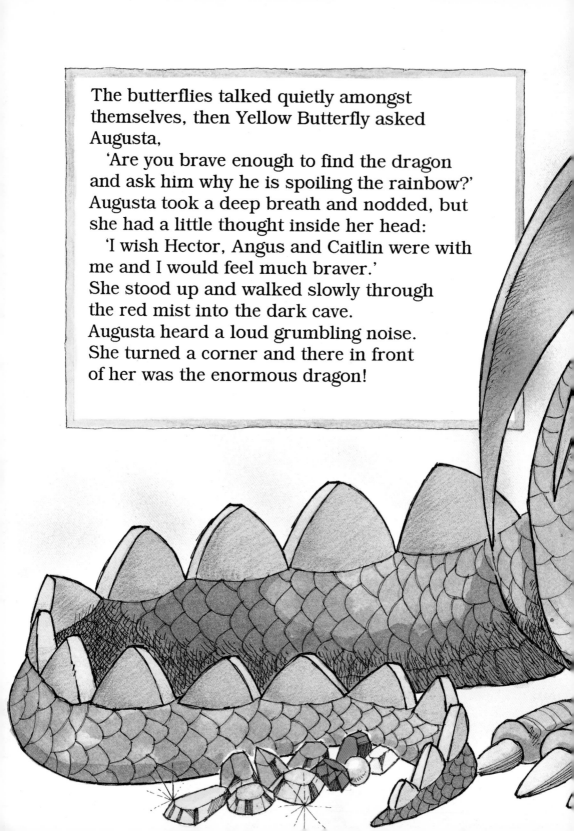

'Who are you?' roared the dragon.
Bravely Augusta answered,
   'I am Augusta Maclean, today's birthday
child. I have come to Birthday Land to find
the end of the rainbow and my special party.
You have forgotten to put my birthstone at the
entrance to your cave.'
She looked around. The sparkle of thousands
of birthstones lit up the cave.
The dragon's scales gleamed. Augusta looked
carefully back at him.
   'Why are you spoiling the rainbow?'
she asked. 'I will not be able to find its end
because of all your fiery red breath.'

The dragon hung his head and a big tear fell from the corner of one eye.

'Augusta,' he said. 'I have lived in Birthday Land for hundreds of years and I've never met a child who shares my birthday.'

Augusta looked surprised.

'No child has ever visited Birthday Land on my birthday,' the dragon continued, 'because it's the only day in the year when all Birthday Land has a special holiday and no child visits.'

'When is your birthday?' Augusta asked the dragon. He gave a big sigh and said in a sad voice,

'The 29th of October.'

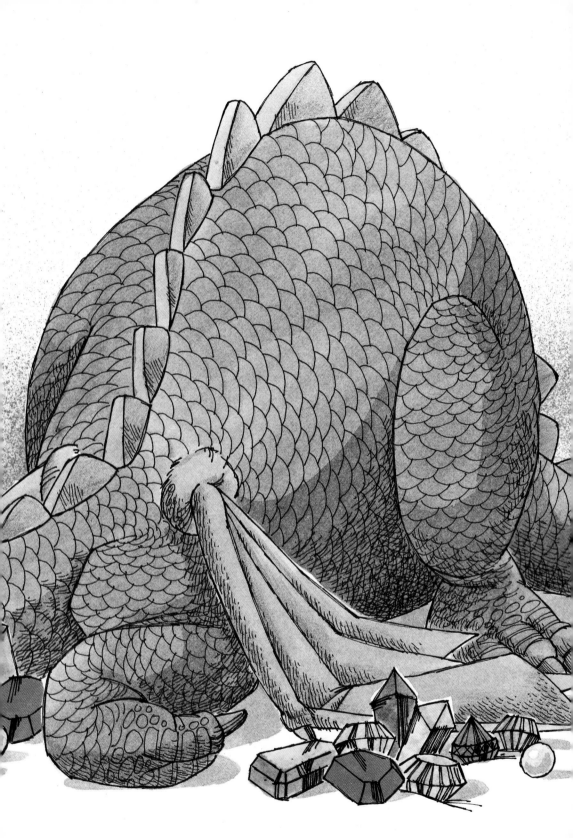

'Why, that's today!' cried Augusta. 'Today is the 29th of October and it's my birthday, too!' The dragon stared at her, then he roared:

'Impossible! No child visits us today. How did you get into Birthday Land?'

'I think the elves were tired of the very red rainbow,' smiled Augusta. 'They wanted a brave birthday child to cheer you up so that the rainbow could get back to its true colours.' The dragon stood up to his full height and laughed,

'What a wonderful birthday this is! From now on I will have someone with whom I can share my birthday!'

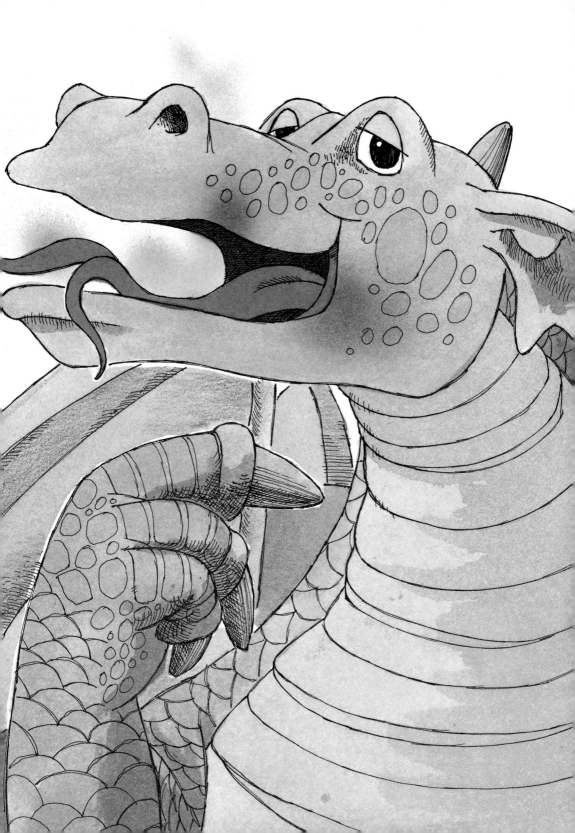

The dragon stretched out a long claw,
picked up one of the special stones and gave
it to Augusta.

'This is an opal,' he said, 'your October
birthstone. Now you can find your birthday
party.'
The happy dragon took Augusta back to the
waiting butterflies.

'Well done, Augusta!' they cried. 'The
dragon is happy and the red mist is
disappearing. Now we'll find the end of the
rainbow!'
The dragon smiled: 'Happy Birthday,
Augusta!'

'Happy Birthday, dragon!' laughed
Augusta as she sat down on the leaf.
The butterflies flew Augusta back towards the
rainbow. All the red mist had disappeared.

'Look, look!' she cried. 'I can see the end
of the rainbow!'

The butterflies pulled Augusta down towards the end of the rainbow. She carefully held her opal and the calendular present. Down below she could just see lots of balloons and streamers and... 'Close your eyes, Augusta,' called the butterflies.

'SURPRISE!' Augusta opened her eyes. And there was the biggest surprise of her birthday. There were lots of people she knew and there amongst them were Hector, Angus and Caitlin! In the middle of the party table was the most wonderful birthday cake in the world. On it was written:

HAPPY

BIRTHDAY

AUGUSTA